Sparkle River

Karina W. Zhang

Dedicated to Hannah M. Wang

Table of Contents

Chapter I
Leopardi's Spell

In 1821, in a forest in the darkest depths of what we now call Hoh Campground, a giant, four-headed leopard emerged from its afternoon nap. It roared a giant roar, and monstrous beasts marched towards it–north, south, east, west–from all corners of the damp forest. They knelt beside the leopard, their slanted, colorful, flame-like eyes glowing in the black mist.

A sleuth of seven-headed bears approached. They growled, "Why did you take our forest, invaders?"

The four-headed leopard didn't answer the question and just let out another great roar, and the monsters beside it started to attack the bears. The bears retreated to the treetops to avoid injuries. It was dark, and the bears couldn't be seen.

"You bully!" Only the angry shout was reverberating in the forest.

The four-headed leopard's youngest servant asked its master, "Q.C Leopardi, should we search the forest for those bears?"

The servant looked like a black wolf, and since its fur was dark like its surroundings, only its green eyes were visible.

Q.C Leopardi, the four-headed leopard, didn't answer the question directly. He started murmuring to cast an evil spell: "Only the beginning of July can outsiders intrude, as we make a trap to turn them into food. If the bears or a dragon is caught, I shall give my servants prizes. If nothing is found in the trap, they'll meet terrible surprises. I won't do anything, even if there's only normal prey. I'll make that all happen in July, the first day."

Over the years, the bears didn't stop their constant fight to get their forest back. However, in the year 1943, on July first, Q.C Leopardi's trap trapped these bears.

Four hours later, a kind hiker named Sylvester Usoro found the bears. For a second, he was frightened because of the bears' many heads, jet-black fur, and extraordinarily long claws. But then, he noticed that the bears were more worried than he was. They thought that Sylvester was going to leave them alone! Sylvester set the bears free and was quite sure that the bears he helped whispered, "Thank you."

He watched the bears leap from stone to stone, heading somewhere that he could not see. Q.C Leopardi heard about the bears being set free. By July first, 2018, the leopard was more solemn about this situation than any other. It would punish its servants severely if there was no food or bear in the trap. But not everyone was as serious.

Meanwhile, outside Clyde Suco's house, the rosy, golden sunlight was constantly trying to pass through Clyde's bedroom's blue, translucent curtains as some nearby songbirds chirped the daily sunrise melody. Clyde woke up; the pretty light and the beautiful song was his annual natural alarm clock. Instead of going back to bed, Clyde pulled aside the curtains, opened the window, and inhaled some fresh morning breeze but exhaled it in an instant. Immediately, the morning's brightness broke in, and Clyde blinked in the light to adjust to it. He shivered. It was just a little chilly. The reason Eight-year-old Clyde was excited was because he and his family were going camping at Hoh Campground that day.

Clyde changed into a pair of black sweatpants, a pair of white socks, a green T-shirt, and a light-gray jacket and rushed downstairs, his brown hair messily flying in the air. He ran to the kitchen as fast as his legs could carry him. He already smelled luscious waffles waiting for him.

Mom and Dad were topping their waffles with whipped cream, maple syrup, and berries while Clyde's nine-year-old sister, Penelope Suco, was still packing. She was wearing green and brown, as she usually dressed during a camping trip. Her brown hair was in a ponytail.

Mom's hair was brown like everyone else's in the family, and she was wearing a white sweater. Dad was wearing his black jacket, and he was the only one with blue eyes out of the rest of the family–they had gray eyes. He had inherited that trait from his father, and his older brother, who was five years older than him, had the same eye color.

Clyde sat down at the breakfast table and put whipped cream and sprinkles on each of his waffles. He said during his sixth serving, "These are so delicious! Can I have more, Mom?"

Mom replied, "Not too much, darling. We need to get going for the camping trip. Make sure to comb your hair, brush your teeth, and wash your face. You're messy. I don't think Penelope has time to eat." She turned to her daughter and asked, "Penelope, honey, how long is it going to take you to pack?"

Penelope replied with a smile, "You can never get too prepared!" She resumed gathering every single one of her emergency supplies. Once she was done packing, Clyde, Penelope, and their parents went to hit the road, but little did they know that the forest near their campsite was the one Q.C Leopardi now lived in—aka, the Forest of Doom and Death.

Around 2:45 p.m., the family arrived at the destination. Dad told the kids, "Go and explore—have some fun, but do not go out of sight. Your mom and I will unpack."

Instead, Clyde and Penelope went out of sight to explore, completely ignoring their dad's advice. Suddenly, they saw a scarlet wave in a big burrow near the forest. They were too curious to see what the wave was.

"Do you think that 'red' read the books you brought?" Penelope joked.

Clyde replied, "Nah, I don't think so."

Clyde and Penelope crawled in. The entrance of the burrow disappeared. Clyde and Penelope were trapped. Clyde pointed at a tunnel. "I think that's the exit. It's also where the red glow is coming from," he pointed out. "Let's go!"

He and Penelope hurtled into the tunnel and out but regretted it at once. The tunnel had vanished, and a wall blocked the edges. The surroundings were forest-like, and the light was dim. The air was stiff. The two stood up, wobbling like gelatin.

Clyde wished that he had not exhaled the fresh morning breeze as quickly, remembering the crisp air back at home. Penelope coughed in the dust. "Look, the red glow! Uh oh, it's lava! IT'S BEHIND YOU!" The air was so stuffy; it was like a major accomplishment for Penelope to talk. It was also hard for Penelope to not be funny.

The lava started to bubble. Clyde and his sister hurtled onto a large stone. When the stone was about to turn into rust because of the hot lava beneath it, Clyde and

Penelope each grasped a vine hanging from a tree above and swung over a canyon in the way, gripping for dear life.

Once they swung across the canyon, the kids ran faster than ever, not wanting to get burnt, but a ten-foot-tall brick wall blocked their path. Clyde gasped. The lava was closing in. It had already overfilled the canyon. Penelope pointed at the wall then at Clyde. She wanted to climb the wall! The two grabbed every ledge in reach and started to climb.

Once they reached the top, the kids slid down a smooth, red, wooden slope that led over the wall, keeping in mind that the lava would eventually turn the wall into rust.

Clyde and Penelope saw a dragon standing two meters away from them.

Clyde began, "We're done for–"

The dragon smiled. He held out a claw for the kids to shake. He whispered, "Hi, my name is Blaze Suco–"

"Hey, that's my cousin's name!" Clyde shouted excitedly. "My name is Clyde–"

"And that's one of my cousins' names too–and please keep your voice down. I'm hiding."

Penelope whispered, "Penelope is my name, but why are you a dragon, not human?"

Blaze replied, "Q.C Leopardi. Dragon blood has healing powers, and you could make an unbreakable cloak out of our hide. I used to be human. Your father's older brother is my father. My parents took me to a campsite near this forest three years ago when I was six. They knew this place was magical and told me to stay near them. But I disobeyed, and I got kidnapped by one of Q.C Leopardi's most devoted servants.

"Q.C Leopardi was deeply hurt at that time because of a sleuth of monstrous bears. Q.C Leopardi used magic and transformed me into a dragon so it can drink my blood and have no injury, along with ripping off my hide for a rag that is unbreakable. But I escaped.

"When I was escaping Q.C Leopardi, the sleuth of bears was mad at it. They love humans. They told me to hide and defend myself while they distracted Q.C Leopardi. So, I've hid for three years now. We should team up."

Penelope said, "But you might be lying."

Penelope took out a flask of potion. She explained, "This is Reliability Potion. The drinker couldn't resist telling the truth. If you really are Blaze, you would know that you gave it to me for my fourth birthday and your parents made the best spaghetti ever. I remember that like the back of my hand."

"I remember, and it was really rainy outside," replied Blaze.

Penelope nodded.

Blaze drank the potion.

Penelope whispered, "Are you honest and trustworthy?"

"Yes," replied Blaze. As he did, the wall started to tumble–the lava had broken it.

Clyde and Penelope climbed onto Blaze's back, and the black dragon took flight, dodging vines, branches, thorns, and Q.C Leopardi's servants. Blaze's dark scales helped camouflaging a lot. They matched Human Blaze's black hair. The servant who kidnapped Blaze–a cougar-like monster that looked like it didn't have any flesh with flame-blue eyes–whispered something unbelievably quiet down below, and Blaze started to grow tired of flying.

The beast servants vanished, each with a villainous smile. Blaze used his wings to safely parachute to the ground. Lava started to close in. An acid lake was in front of them.

Clyde recalled Blaze saying that nothing could break a dragon's hide. He gestured Blaze to swim across the acid lake, knowing that the lava was deep enough to burn Penelope and himself.

Blaze swam with Clyde and Penelope on board. Once across the lake, Q.C Leopardi was standing only a few meters away from them. It whispered to some beasts, "Ah, I see, unless I am blind, that we have a dream come true. A fresh, delicious meal waiting for us, including kids and a dragon. Excellent job, my friends. The trap finally worked. I hope they lure the bears. We can have a feast!" Only the greedy monsters could hear that.

Q.C Leopardi stomped, and various other monsters came for their eighteenth snack of the day. "Dig in!" Q.C Leopardi shouted.

Blaze breathed fire at each of the incoming monsters to defend his cousins. Clyde and Penelope knew what to do: they threw sticks, dirt, pebbles, and stones at Q.C Leopardi.

Within five minutes, the only monsters in sight were Blaze and Q.C Leopardi. Clyde's brain suddenly sparked an idea. He whispered it to Blaze. Blaze nodded and started to act like he needed help badly.

A growl echoed through the forest.

The sleuth of seven-headed bears came and started to fight Q.C Leopardi. The sleuth knew that, since humans have saved them, they had to save humans–for the second time. The monstrous bears slashed their long claws at Q.C Leopardi, who tried to smash the bears, but Clyde noticed that Q.C Leopardi has weakened over the years. With another great slash, the bears ripped off some fur from Q.C Leopardi. After five minutes, Q.C Leopardi and the bears crumbled in dust. It turned out that the four-headed leopard and the sleuth of bears lived over their species' lifespan, and they were too old to hold up the injuries.

On the bright side, Blaze transformed back into his nine-year-old self, wearing a gray sweatshirt and blue pants. The forest light grew brighter, and the nature was less damp. The lava turned into a rainbow. The acid lake turned into a sparkly river. The dust turned into moss. Air was fresh. Leopardi's spell was broken.

Clyde, Penelope, and Blaze walked out of the forest. The entrance, which they used as an exit, was open. Clyde and Penelope went to meet their parents at the campsite. Blaze followed them.

When they saw their son and daughter, Mom and Dad ran to them and hugged them, asking them many questions about what happened and describing how worried they were. They were surprised to see Blaze, but he just said, "To make a long story short, we shouldn't ignore our parents' advice!"

Clyde gave a thumbs-up.

"After all that... oh, wow, it's evening already," Dad gasped.

They ate some cabbage, pork, carrots, and bread. After they finished, Mom smiled, "Well, all of us deserve marshmallows!"

"Yay!" shouted everyone else, and they had fun...until *night*.

Chapter II
The Sky and the Water

As the family roasted marshmallows, they told spooky stories under the moonlight. Dad said in a low, creepy voice to match the scene of his tale, "One dark night, a few villagers were traveling in the black mist until they saw a pair of red eyes glaring at them."

Clyde knew how it felt in wicked fog; he still remembered how the Forest of Doom and Death looked like.

Dad continued, "A ghostly, green claw reached for the fruits in the villagers' baskets. The villagers screamed, 'Help me, some–'"

"–Wait," interrupted Blaze. "Where is Penelope?"

The fire went out. Clyde, the youngest, shivered. Was it because he was cold without the campfire's heat or scared without the campfire's light? A shadow leaned over him.

"Boo!" said the figure, who was Penelope. She looked at Clyde, who jumped into the tent without a word and giggled. "Clyde, it's just me!" Penelope laughed.

"Penelope!" said Clyde, who noticed that he had discovered something that his family had not seen. "There's a wolf-like shadow leaning over you!"

Penelope lit the campfire to see what was going on behind her. She turned around and stepped forward. She shrieked and ran into the tent with Blaze behind her.

Dad and Mom looked around, willing to defend the kids. Suddenly, they fainted.

Once again, the adventure was on.

"There m-must b-be a n-new villain," said Blaze in a trembling voice. "The f-friendly bears al-already d-defeated Q.C Leopardi, s-so there must b-be s-someone else."

Clyde shivered. "I brought a book that may help," and he took out a book entitled Harry Potter and the Sorcerer's Stone.

"It wouldn't help," sighed Penelope. "The third book of Harry Potter has a werewolf in it, which I think was the shadow, but you didn't bring it."

Blaze suddenly sprang up. "That's it!" he whispered. "When I was five and a half years old, my parents took me to a dig site. I dug deep and found an old book with runes. I'm learning to read runes at Magician Hills Academy. I never bothered to read the book since I hated Earth Magic–until now."

Blaze took out the book and read the title, Magical Creature Explorer's Guide, and the first page's heading, "Trolls." He interrupted himself and said, "Not useful. How about…" He flipped to another page and read, "Werewolves."

Clyde and Penelope listened and curled up in the tent.

Blaze continued: "'Known to have no tail, werewolves are half-man, half-wolf. At night or during a full moon, they transform into a wolf-like form. During the daytime, they remain in human form. Whoever gets bitten by this nasty beast will turn into one themself. The most harmful one goes by the name Wolf-Eye Scratch. Werewolves are afraid of silver and wolfsbane, so it is best to have some of each when you are camping in Hoh Campground in 2018. That way, you can kill a werewolf with a silver bullet or knife. Some werewolves were born a werewolf, not bitten like Wolf-Eye.'"

Clyde asked, "Blaze, who's the author? I didn't know that Wolf-Eye Scratch was a name."

Penelope said, "Find out quickly. I'm a bit nervous to trust things, and books can't drink Reliability Potion without a mouth."

Blaze replied, "The name of the author doesn't look like runes."

It was true, the author's name was not like the text of the book. In fact, it was like English, but a code replaced the name: X22-6•D1-7. Penelope glanced at Mom and Dad, who were still lying motionless on the floor.

Blaze said, "My parents are magical. They have said something about Sparkle River, the only river with water that has the power to cure faints. My parents know where Sparkle River is but said that it was too dangerous along the way–the fact we have to face the Dread."

"Sounds like they would be an immense help," said Clyde. "Right now, it's too dark to travel. Keep the campfire on while we sleep." Clyde didn't know about the Dread, but it sounded like you couldn't take a plane to the river.

Penelope roasted some food the best she could and ate quickly with the kids. They took turns changing into new clothes in the tent. Since Blaze didn't have clothes to change into, he just went into the tent after his cousins finished so he could sleep with them.

That night, Clyde had a dream:

"I have a present for you!" Dream-Mom said. She handed Dream-Clyde a watch. Dream-Dad explained, "Click the red button, and who you want to appear will appear. Click the blue button to turn humans that were bitten by werewolves back into a human. The screen of your watch has X-ray vision. It also shows time."

Clyde woke up to find part of his dream true. He did have a watch with two buttons. He crawled out of his sleeping bag and woke up the rest. He explained his dream and the miracle that happened after it.

Blaze said, "Weird, I had a dream that I could transform into anything I want, and now I can turn into a human, dragon, cheetah, and a dolphin whenever I want to."

"Same with me," said Penelope. "I could draw something, and it would become real like in my dream. When I drew flowers, they became real. But when I drew Sparkle River water, it turned into normal water."

Clyde exclaimed, "Let's pack before our voyage to the River of Sparkles!"

Penelope used a stick and drew a big suitcase on the dirt. As it became real, Penelope drew food, paper, other important things, and a burden of water. She made sure to draw mimics of everyone's clothes, hand sanitizer, sanitizing wipes, and deodorant (she still wanted everyone to be clean).

Clyde pressed the red button on his watch, and Blaze's parents appeared, each with magic wands, prepared and knowing what to do. Clyde and Penelope hugged Uncle Drone, who looked like a taller version of Blaze with longer hair, and Aunt Virgo, who had the same hair color and eyes as her husband.

They started asking about what happened to their precious son and explaining how they couldn't break into the Forest of Doom and Death. They were both wearing indigo robes. Uncle Drone's had stars on it, and Aunt

Virgo's was longer. They were relieved when the kids told them that their worst injury was only a cut rather than a broken bone or something.

Clyde lifted the water bottles, food, the packed-up tent, and the Magical Creature Explorer's Guide into the suitcase as Blaze transformed into a dragon, ready to carry the suitcase, Penelope, and Clyde.

They ate the remaining food that Mom and Dad packed for the trip and flew up into the sky. Blaze's mother and father kicked off their broomsticks and were flying in the air with the kids in no time.

Uncle Drone said, "North from here, until you see the ocean. Blaze, your mother will tell you the directions when we arrive."

Aunt Virgo led the way with Uncle Drone circling around the kids, ready to knock out anything in the way. Aunt Virgo called out, "We might need to stop in the middle, because a storm will come at noon, everyone!" She led the group to a nearby clearing.

Uncle Drone said, "A tent won't work in a storm–fortunately, this clearing is sandy, not muddy or grassy, so Penelope, I hope you don't mind drawing a safe house."

Penelope got off Blaze and drew a house (windowless house, that is–lightning can break windows): a lockable black door, a strong roof, lights, couches, beds, a kitchen, a pantry, and a bookshelf. It became reality as Penelope opened the door.

Aunt Virgo suggested, "Let's name ourselves 'the Searchers of Life' so it's easier to call everyone without names." Everybody agreed. Clyde and the rest of the Searchers of Life went inside. Aunt Virgo and Penelope made lunch.

After half an hour, Penelope called, "Lunchtime!"

Clyde went downstairs and ate the food: chicken, spinach, rice, and bananas. Even though lunch was not Blaze's favorite, he preferred having this rather than starving.

Once the Searchers of Life finished their lunch, Uncle Drone and Aunt Virgo told the kids to be in the playroom of the house to pass the time. Clyde gave Penelope a piece of paper that she had drawn previously as he said, "Draw a couch in this playroom. We should rest for a bit."

Penelope drew a couch and hopped onto its fluffy pillows. Clyde was after her, but Blaze was borrowing Clyde's watch to watch the storm, remembering that the house was windowless.

"The storm is about over," declared Blaze, handing Clyde's watch back. Clyde looked at the screen of his watch and found out that Blaze was right.

The storm turned into a shower. The shower turned into rain. The rain turned into a drizzle, and the drizzle stayed how it was.

Clyde pressed the red button on his watch, and Uncle Drone and Aunt Virgo appeared. "Even though we might get a bit wet, we can resume our journey," said Uncle Drone.

The Searchers of Life followed him out and repacked their things. Blaze turned into a dragon, ready for takeoff. The Searchers of Life got in their positions and took off into the sky.

Blaze and his parents flew higher and higher into the sky. Clyde gripped harder, fearing falling off. Penelope thought it was bizarre to be over the clouds.

Aunt Virgo led the Searchers of Life into a sandy clearing when it looked like Blaze was tired. She asked, "Penelope, could you please draw two jetpacks for you and your brother so you guys could fly? My son is a bit tired of carrying luggage and humans."

Penelope drew jetpacks, and she and Clyde put them on.

"New positioning!" shouted Uncle Drone, but his voice was faint because the wind was still roaring louder than a lion. "I lead, my wife is the caboose, circling around you kids. Blaze, you be in the middle of your cousins. Penelope on the left, Clyde on the right. Ready? Takeoff!"

The Searchers of Life obeyed and soared even higher into the sky. Very fat raindrops fell on Clyde's head. There were very few, but sometimes they would blow into their eye because of the rain. After four hours of flying, the Searchers of Life arrived at the Ocean.

Uncle Drone said, "It's 5:30 p.m., and it isn't a bad idea to camp out for a while down at that campsite, near the ocean. Nowhere to draw, though."

Clyde and the rest got the tent set up—it was better than sleeping on cold rocks and sand. Clyde and Blaze got the firewood, remembering about werewolves. Penelope helped Uncle Drone and Aunt Virgo roll out the sleeping bags inside the tent.

After the fire was lit, Aunt Virgo found some food in the suitcase: beef, BBQ sauce, and bread. They roasted, and they ate, and Blaze turned back into human form. The Searchers of Life took their shoes off and crawled into the tent.

Aunt Virgo went into her purple sleeping bag, Uncle Drone in his midnight-blue one, Blaze in his black one, Penelope in her magenta one, and Clyde in his turquoise one. They slept sweetly—if you do not count Clyde.

Chapter III
Friend of the Sea

That night, Clyde had a nightmare. "Wake up, Clyde!" shouted Dream-Penelope. "There's a tsunami!" When Dream-Clyde got out of the tent, it was too late. He was dead.

At that moment, Clyde woke up to find out that there were big waves last night, but he was lucky to find himself on Blaze's dolphin-mode back with Penelope. At least it's sunny now, Clyde thought.

Uncle Drone and Aunt Virgo were flying in the air on their broomsticks, carrying the suitcase, looking tired. Clyde looked at his watch, scanning the ocean floor for sharks, lionfish, stingrays, and other harmful sea creatures. Blaze turned into a dragon and flew up towards his parents, getting into his old position.

Blaze said, "Sorry, Clyde. The jetpacks Penelope drew fell into the water during the high tide."

"It's okay," said Clyde, who was still weary of deadly animals. "It's not your fault."

Penelope changed the topic as she whispered, "The ocean is a long place to travel, and we can't get our tent set up in the ocean! We didn't even get breakfast, and I need to go to the bathroom!"

Clyde laughed at the word "bathroom," but Blaze murmured, "It's not funny when it's happening." Clyde smelled the chilly morning air. There wasn't so much fog. It smelled like...salt.

Uncle Drone cast a spell on Penelope so that she would not need to go to the bathroom for eighty minutes. Uncle Drone and Aunt Virgo were still in search of a place to rest but had no luck.

After one hour, Aunt Virgo finally said, "There's an island."

The Searchers of Life soared down to the island, unsure if it was safe or not. They were lucky to find it sandy and full of vegetable patches and fruit trees. Penelope drew a strong house to make sure tsunamis would not break it.

Suddenly, a man with long nails and slits for pupils appeared. Penelope and Clyde screamed as they ran into the house with Blaze. This man wasn't ordinary–he was a werewolf in human form!

Uncle Drone and Aunt Virgo looked at the werewolf with their wands drawn up. The werewolf looked bloody. His clothes were like rags with rips and bloodstains all over. His messy hair and eye color were red like blood.

He said, "Hi. I've been searching for a friend."

Penelope opened a window from inside the house and threw Reliability Potion into Uncle Drone's hands, gesturing him to pour some into the werewolf's mouth.

Uncle Drone poured a bit into the werewolf's mouth and asked, "Who are you? Are you evil? And what is your history?"

The werewolf replied, "I am Goldstain Hulls. I couldn't, like all werewolves, control myself in wolf form.

"When I was born, I was a human. A werewolf named Wolf-Eye Scratch bit me, and before I knew it, I was a werewolf at age seven.

"At age ten, I joined the other werewolves to see if they could make friends with me, but they were evil. Still no friends for me.

"At age fourteen, I learned that werewolves were afraid of silver and wolfsbane. Never even went near any of those things. But luckily, a sleuth of bears and a whale called Moby Dick were willing to make friends with me.

"At age twenty-one, my friends, the seven-headed bears, died partly from age. Yesterday was my birthday, so now I'm twenty-three years old."

"Happy late birthday!" shouted Clyde, who finally decided to run outside. "Do you know why our mother and father fainted?"

Goldstain said, "Yes, I do. I was battling Wolf-Eye, who nearly killed your parents. He punched me hard since I got in the way, but your parents only fainted. That's why I have so many bloodstains."

Penelope quickly drew a giftbox with a card inside and handed it to Goldstain.

"'Dear Goldstain,'" Goldstain read. "'Happy (late) birthday! We can be friends if you want! Would you rather be human or werewolf? Love, your new friends.'"

Goldstain said, "Human."

"Sure thing!" said Blaze. Clyde pressed the blue button on his watch as Goldstain turned into a human. His red eye slits were no longer there–only pupils with green eyes. His nails were shorter.

The Searchers of Life introduced themselves.

Goldstain asked, "Why are you guys here, anyway?"

Aunt Virgo explained, "Clyde and Penelope's parents fainted, and we need Sparkle River water. You know that rock? It won't appear in front of us at the Hollow Fir unless we feel the Dread."

Clyde was confused about the rock and the fir, but he asked no question.

Goldstain replied, "Oh, I see. I can help. No worries!"

The Searchers of Life let Goldstain be a member of the Searchers of Life. They noticed that he was a good climber and gardener when he climbed a tree and got a coconut.

Suddenly, a rabbit came along, trying to steal the ripe carrots. Goldstain spoke an unknown language, and the rabbit seemed to understand.

The rabbit took only three carrots out of the fifteen, and the Searchers of Life noticed that their new friend could speak Rabbit.

"I'm starving," complained Clyde. "It's 9:15 and no breakfast!"

"Don't worry," Goldstain said with a smile. "Find a lot of apples so I can make apple pie."

The kids smacked their lips and ran off into an apple orchard. Aunt Virgo made the rest of the food while her spouse went fishing for fish.

Clyde climbed a tree and found a few ripe apples. Penelope shook a tree as apples came falling into her basket. Blaze transformed into a cheetah and ran around the orchard, pouncing on falling apples.

At last, Clyde said, "I got fifty-nine apples!"

Penelope said, "Great, let's go back and have breakfast!"

Blaze turned back into a human and joined his parents along with his cousins and werewolf friend.

Goldstain went into the house and baked pie.

"I already smell something aromatic and luscious! Goldstain really is good at baking pie," said Blaze said, sniffing the air.

Penelope giggled her usual giggle as she joked, "You can't bake pi! You can't bake 3.14159265358979323... Wait, what?"

"All I can remember is 3.14, um, 1," said Clyde.

Blaze said, "I can memorize." He took a deep breath and said at top speed, "3.14159265358979323846264338327950288416716939937510 8."

"Whoa, slow down, pal," said Goldstain. "If you're out of breath, you can't eat anymore pie or pi."

He held up the delicious pie and a strip of some of the digits of pi Blaze did not memorize.

"Who cares?" asked Clyde. "Let's have pie–pi– already!"

Aunt Virgo cut the pie into sixths so everyone could get the same amount. Clyde, Penelope, and Blaze finished their slices within a minute, loving the taste and wishing for more.

Goldstain saw the expression on their faces, feeling sorry for them. He said, "More apples, more pie. More brains, more pi. If you get milk, vanilla extract, and ice, you can have ice cream to go with the pie."

Blaze transfigured himself into a cheetah and ran into the orchard. Penelope went to a cow Goldstain owned and started to milk the cow. Aunt Virgo and Uncle Drone got water from the ocean and used magic to take out the salt and freeze the water into ice.

Goldstain told Clyde, "See that golden gate? It leads to magical herbs. Pick a few of the white and golden ones called Vanict Blossoms and put them into the dinosaur-like plant, Spice Graizers. You will get vanilla extract."

Clyde did what he was told. He opened the golden gate and gasped. Not a frightened gasp, a surprised gasp. Not a surprised gasp of something terrible, but a surprised gasp of amazement. Absolutely pure amazement.

There was a beautiful garden. There was a marble fountain with sparkly water. The water in the fountain was warm.

Clyde picked a few Vanict Blossoms, put them into a nearby Spice Graizer, and put the vanilla extract into a small Grip 'n' Seal Ziploc.

He decided to explore the garden. He found a hidden, golden door in around some welcoming plants that chanted, "Welcome to one! Welcome to all! Welcome at winter, spring, summer, and fall!"

It was not the door Clyde had come in from.

There were two gargoyles guarding the door. They growled, "Go. You are not Goldstain, which means you can't go in."

Clyde did not want to get into a battle with moving statues, so he backed off, out of the gate entrance, and back to Goldstain. He handed him the Ziploc with the vanilla extract.

Goldstain said, "Perfect! You can go to the pool to clean yourself while I make ice cream and pie. The pool is just around the corner of the orchard."

Clyde looked at himself. He was dirty. He thought, It wouldn't hurt to take a bath!

Clyde ran to the pool and cleaned his hands in the cool, sparkly water with the rest of the kids with him. He plunged into the water and cleaned his face.

He grabbed some of the dirty clothes he wore previously on the journey and started to wash them. Penelope helped Clyde wrap the clean clothes in Silxtrea silk.

Blaze said, "Goldstain explained that Slixtrea produces silk and traps heat from the sun in the silk, making any wet things wrapped in the silk dry."

The kids heard Uncle Drone cry, "Now let's get a move on!"

The kids ran back to the house. There, they saw Goldstain making a weird whale bellow. Aunt Virgo seemed satisfied with it. A few minutes later, a whale came.

"Goldstain could speak Whale?!" asked Penelope.

Uncle Drone patted her back and said, "Yes, he can. He's telling Moby Dick to move this island to China, the place with Sparkle River, though no Chinese people know about it."

Moby Dick gently carried the island towards Shanghai, China, but of course it would still be a long ride. (He went at a slow speed, making sure no one fell if he went too fast.) After three hours, the Searchers of Life decided to make lunch. It was 12:15 p.m., and lunch was needed.

Goldstain, Aunt Virgo, and Penelope went inside the house to make food. Uncle Drone went to the pool to pick up the kids' clothes. Only Blaze and Clyde were left. "I'm bored," Clyde complained, yawning.

Blaze suggested, "How about playing Chopsticks?"

"It's too classic to me, and it could go on forever!" Clyde pointed out the disadvantages.

"How about swimming with Moby Dick? You could turn into a dolphin and carry me!"

"But you couldn't breathe underwater," Blaze reminded Clyde.

Clyde said, "Penelope could draw scuba gear. You don't need three people making lunch."

"Penelope said that she was making something too special for just two people to make."

Clyde decided to try it anyway. When he entered the kitchen, Goldstain said, "We're too busy, Clyde, but you could have this slip so the gargoyles will let you into my house." He gave Clyde a golden slip with the golden words:

I can enter the golden door,

stepping onto Goldstain's floor.

I am doing this to pass the time,

oh, gargoyles, won't you be kind?

Or Goldstain says that he'll get mad...

don't start begging, "Please, my lad.

-GOLDSTAIN HULLS

Blaze exclaimed, "Amazing! Let's go to Goldstain's house! I wonder what Goldstain meant about Goblin Mine."

"Sounds like a mine with goblins," muttered Clyde. Together, they ran into the golden gates, past the beautiful fountain, and to the gargoyles.

The Welcoming Plants chanted, "Welcome to one! Welcome to all! Welcome at winter, spring, summer, and fall!" which now grew annoying. The gargoyles looked at Clyde's slip.

They shivered at the words "Goblin Mine" and let Clyde and Blaze in. They went into a silver elevator with fake diamonds on the side.

Clyde looked at the buttons below the mirror in the elevator. "Buttons with a bed, oven, toy truck, computer, telescope, television, tree, clay, snorkel, pencil, book, and globe. Probably the one with the snorkel would do the trick."

Blaze clicked it. "Glad he didn't have thirteen buttons," he said as the elevator slowly moved down. "My mom said it was unlucky!"

"Oh, yeah," agreed Clyde.

A minute later, the elevator door slid open. The floor it led to was made from glass. Under the glass was the ocean and Moby Dick's back. It was gray.

Clyde heard a faint "Ready! The pie with ice cream is ready plus something special!"

Blaze thought it was his own imagination, and Clyde thought it was Blaze playing a prank. Clyde put on the smallest scuba gear on a shelf. He hoped to have fun, since time flies–perhaps swims–when you're having fun.

Chapter IV
Goblins and an Elf

Blaze said, "Perfect!" as he transformed into a dolphin with Clyde on his back. The glass floor opened, and Clyde and Blaze swam into the water and found Moby Dick waving to them cheerfully.

The glass floor closed. Surprisingly, no water was let in.

Blaze, as a dolphin, was a type of whale, only able to speak Whale in dolphin mode.

To Clyde, Blaze was making a weird squeaking noise, but Blaze, since he was in dolphin mode, heard himself squeaking, "Hi, Moby Dick! Do you know how long it will take to arrive at Shanghai?"

"I don't really know," came Moby Dick's bellow as reply.

"It's okay! Maybe you'll find out!"

After the little conversation, Blaze translated what Moby Dick was saying to Clyde so he could understand.

Suddenly, Clyde waved his arms up and down. As he waved, he grew frantic.

Blaze knew that there was something dangerous up ahead, so he told Moby Dick in Whale, "An island up ahead! Stop swimming! We need to make sure no one will sneak up on us when you turn!"

Moby Dick stopped swimming.

Suddenly, a hand tapped Clyde's shoulder. It was Goldstain, holding his breath, gesturing the boys to go back onto land. He needed to tell them something.

"There's an island up ahead," Goldstain explained when Blaze was back into human form on land. "We could explore–after more breakfast."

Clyde gave Goldstain the scuba gear and gobbled up the pie and ice cream, ending up with a brain-freeze.

"I wish I could have tiramisu cheesecake, though," muttered Clyde. Blaze agreed, "Tiramisu cheesecake doesn't do much harm."

Penelope told them, "That's the surprise! Who doesn't love tiramisu cheesecake?"

The kids and adults ate the cheesecake, and when they were finished, they took turns going into the bathroom and putting on swimsuits that Penelope had drawn and got off Goldstain's home island and swam to But-Still Island. The current was small.

When they reached the island, a little elf, who was only as tall as a large computer screen, waved to the Searchers of Life.

"You look cheerful," said Aunt Virgo. The elf squeaked, "That's what Kiwi said, but still."

"Blaze's mother's name is not But-Still," said Penelope, who thought the elf meant Aunt Virgo's name was But-Still. The elf roared with laughter and said, "That's what Kiwi said, but still!"

His pointy ears and ragged shoes flapped in the wind as his little hands clutched his chest in humor.

Clyde grew annoyed. He shouted in top speed, "THIS IS NOT A JOKE, LITTLE PERSON WITH POINTY EARS, AND

WE ARE NOT HERE TO LAUGH AT WHATEVER YOU HAVE TO SAY!"

The elf covered his ears at the noise.

After he noticed it was gone, he said weakly, "Fine. Kiwi was trying to annoy you guys so you guys you would turn back, because... GOBLIN MINE IS UP AHEAD, AND IT'S HUNTING TIME FOR THE GOBLINS OF BUT-STILL!"

Aunt Virgo whispered in dismay, "Dang it!" Uncle Drone gasped, and Goldstain covered his mouth and called to Moby Dick, saying to be cautious for the Goblins of But-Still are known to swim and harm whales.

Uncle Drone ordered the kids to hide since they were not fast swimmers. He turned them invisible just in case. Barefooted, the Searchers of Life scrambled to good hiding spots with the elf following Goldstain.

The elf tried to convince Goldstain that he was innocent, but sometimes had his own weird ways of doing things. "Kiwi knows Kiwi was annoying, but at least you know it's hunting time!" the elf remarked.

Goldstain considered the dilemma. He said after a couple minutes, "You can stay. Just try not to be too annoying. But maybe you could annoy our opponents..."

Goldstain had persuaded himself to let the elf stay. When he told the elf his name, his decision, the journey, and the fact that he could join the Searchers of Life and all, the elf said, "Kiwi loves Goldstain! Kiwi thinks Goldstain is the best!"

"Who's Kiwi?" Blaze asked. "Or do you mean the fruit?"

"I'm Kiwi!" said the elf. "Kiwi loves kiwi, so that's why Kiwi's name is Kiwi! How many is are in that?" Clyde knew it was partly an answer to Blaze's question, partly a riddle.

Clyde ran into the bush where the elf was hiding and sighed, "I can't keep track!"

"Zero! Zero!" Penelope cut in from behind a tree.

Kiwi said, "Penelope is right! In the word 'that,' there are no is! Penelope knew Kiwi's trick! Penelope is smart!"

Kiwi said another riddle, "Sam's mother had five children: Mercury, Venus, Earth, Mars, and __. Who is the fifth child?"

"Jupiter, although it's weird for a name," replied Clyde.

"Wrong," said Kiwi.

"I know," Penelope said. "The answer is Sam."

"Ding, ding, ding!" said Kiwi. "In the beginning, Pickle–"

Poison-green flames made their way out of a cave on But-Still Island. Creatures with bare chests and feet carried torches, spears, swords, and shields.

They each wore an ugly rag around their hips with a nasty smile. Their eyes were sharp and caught the Searchers of Life (it took some time). The goblins' pointy ears were like Kiwi's, except much less cheerful.

In fact, the ears looked grumpy, fearsome, evil, and extremely wicked. Goldstain made a signal to be quiet.

At last came the fat king, sitting on his throne with four armored goblins carrying him. His hooked claws clutched a spear full of fire, his lime-green skin glowing in the light.

The armored goblins put the throne down and stood in a horizontal line in front of it. One of them cackled, "I smell something! Ingredients to King Skull's second favorite dish, homo hot dog, probably." The goblins followed the Searchers of Life's scent, and even when some tried to flee and fly away, the goblins were too fast.

If he could think, Blaze would've turned into a cheetah, ran, and when he was far away, he could fly and think of a plan to rescue his friends. But he panicked. When you panic, you can't think. And Blaze got captured because he freaked out.

He, even as a dragon, struggled to get out of a fat, yellowish goblin's grip. That goblin was fatter than King Skull! Clyde was held by a tall goblin with slimy hands–it was the least pleasant experience.

Fortunately, Uncle Drone managed to loosen the goblin's grip with his wand and wiggled out of the largest, most evil-looking goblin's clutches holding Kiwi.

Uncle Drone turned Kiwi and himself into a stone to trick the goblins. Aunt Virgo managed to do the same, but

46

the other poor wandless ones had to stay tickled by the hairs on the goblins.

Goldstain was squeezed lightly by a big, hairy goblin. The goblin wore a skull helmet and had rocks tied to its knees. Penelope was held by an extremely stinky goblin that was three quarters the size of the goblin Goldstain was slightly tortured by.

Both goblins had spikey rock "bracelets" on both hands and rocks tied to their muddy elbows. Those two goblins were both lime-green and had claws that were not sharp or long.

That meant Penelope and Goldstain were safe from scratches! But they could not relax, even with that piece of good news.

Clyde, Penelope, Blaze, and Goldstain had a terrible, unpleasant time with the goblins, hoping to be saved from the nasty creatures.

Aunt Virgo transfigured into herself, but the goblins took no notice (they were gone). Uncle Drone revealed himself bchind Aunt Virgo, carrying Kiwi.

Whispering, whispering, and more whispering. The three really needed to make sure of their plans to save their loved ones.

Just imagine how much cleverness Uncle Drone, Aunt Virgo, and elf needed to have just to save their friends and family. Anything could fail in a case like this!

After Kiwi brought up the invisibility idea, Aunt Virgo remarked, "Don't you remember when they caught us invisible earlier?" Kiwi nodded, but he wasn't done talking.

"One goblin has a good nosy, so does the rest. Let's cover up our scent!"

"Yes, true, it's risky, so everything is good except how we'll sneak in there," explained Uncle Drone. "It's probably where the Goblins of But-Still put their food and all and find gold there for that king."

"Invisibility is the best out of the rest is what Kiwi thinks!" said Kiwi. "There is a 10% chance we won't be caught, and Kiwi knows this island well. Kiwi knows the herb here that covers up smell, Kronkul, on the other side of this small island. I hide there all the time."

48

"Kiwi is right," said Uncle Drone. "Even though the chance we will survive is little, it's more than 0%. But I do expect Clyde to press that helpful red button on his watch."

"Okay, but let's be extra careful," said Aunt Virgo. "And yes, Clyde would probably press the red button."

Kiwi led his friends to a secret path that goblins say is "too clean to waste time to go into" and covered themselves with the Kronkul.

The Kronkuls were bushed with huge heart-shaped, green leaves and tiny pink, white, yellow, or blue flowers that looked like lotus, except they smelled really, really good.

Goblins could only smell food and never could detect fragrances. That was good.

But that was when Uncle Drone, Aunt Virgo, and Kiwi noticed it: what if Clyde, Penelope, Blaze, and Goldstain were eaten already? The three headed ran quickly but quietly towards Goblin Mine, invisible.

Chapter V
Prisoners

At Goblin Mine, it was dark like the Forest of Doom and Death. Clyde, Penelope, Blaze, and Goldstain were cuffed with rusty chains and locked in the same cave. The goblins were getting pieces of steak to use as buns for the homo hot dogs from a storage room.

Blaze was able to breathe fire, as a dragon, to generate a bit of light. Cheetah Blaze's teeth were able to bite off Clyde and Penelope's chains, but no one else was freed from the cuffs.

Clyde and Penelope could only loosen Blaze and Goldstain's chains. Clyde didn't want to trap his aunt and uncle, so he crossed his fingers in the hope they had a plan. Of course, he didn't notice Uncle Drone and Aunt Virgo loosening the lock with their wands.

They quietly crept into the cave with Kiwi. They turned visible. Clyde, Penelope, Blaze, and Goldstain nearly had a heart attack. But they knew that this was good news.

Aunt Virgo and Uncle Drone told Penelope to write the word "escape" on the floor of the prison. A rock appeared. Uncle Drone whispered, "Touch the rock in a 3, in a 2, in a 1!" The Searchers of Life touched the rock.

The Searchers of Life had teleported back onto their island. Uncle Drone used a spell to make a gate go around the island. Aunt Virgo used a spell to make it so Moby Dick could fly and go without water for a century. Moby Dick flew.

The wind whistled in Clyde's ears. The hot sun shined on his back. The smell of salty seawater had returned. After everyone changed into their normal clothes, Goldstain declared, "I'll make lunch!"

After a while, Goldstain exclaimed, "Let's eat!" The Searchers of Life walked towards the table. Blaze said, "The aroma is great!" as he sniffed the air. He was able to make out what was for lunch blindfolded: cabbage, mutton, burritos, sushi, and salmon.

"There's sushi!" said Clyde. "It's my favorite edible thing after tiramisu cheesecake!"

"Same with me!" everyone else agreed. As they ate, Kiwi heard some rustling against the wind. Rain started to pour and ruin the sunshine.

"In the distance, there's something red flying at us," remarked Goldstain, squinting his eyes. "It has horns, a spear-like thing, and razor-sharp teeth. There is also a large green thing flying a couple feet higher."

"I know what they are!" said Clyde, who was interested in fantasy books. "Uh-oh, the first is an *Oni* and the second is an ogre!" The stinky ogre was as large as Moby Dick. It grabbed the massive whale and threw him into the water.

The island had no support.

It spun and spun as it fell from the sky.

Clyde closed his eyes, hoping to open them and find that it was only a nightmare. BANG! BANG! The noise filled his ears. He heard a faint "Quick!" But the bang was too loud for Clyde.

The island fell so quickly that Clyde could not feel the ground.

Suddenly, something made him float in the air instead of falling. There were fewer bangs. He could finally hear words: Penelope spluttering, "Are y-you okay?"; Goldstain gasping, "Who saved us?"; and Aunt Virgo asking, "What was that?"

Clyde finally decided to open his eyes. The rest of the Searchers of Life were also floating like him. Uncle Drone and Aunt Virgo managed to take hold of their brooms. Blaze looked down and saw that Goldstain's island sank.

"I would be sad if my house sank," he muttered sadly. "But at least we're safe!"

Down below, the Oni and ogre were dead, their motionless body lying on But-Still Island.

The happy goblins were munching on them, laughing with their mouths full, "That legendary human killed our prey! The king's absolute favorite, Double O Combo! Mm..."

Kiwi said, "Phew! At least Kiwi knows that Kiwi and Kiwi's friends are safe for now!"

"Okay, seriously, do any of you know where we are?" asked Penelope solemnly, which was different from her usual spirit.

Aunt Virgo had an answer to Penelope's question: "A bit more than halfway across the ocean."

Clyde said, "I think we might make it to the River of Sparkles without dying! We've already escaped death two times in a row–" He was interrupted by a *WHOOSH!* sound.

"A ghoul!" yelled Blaze in fear.

Clyde said, "On second thought, no, we're not going to make it alive."

POOF! Magic dust filled the sky. Coughing, Clyde opened his eyes and blinked. He wondered if he did open his eyes because wherever he was, there was no light.

The surroundings were darker than black. He felt Kiwi's little head but could not tell if it was Kiwi.

After a few minutes, twelve torches lit up. It was the biggest number you could count to by 1s without saying "thirteen." Twelve creepy faces glowed in the firelight: a zombie, skeleton, ghost, mummy, ghoul, draugr, the Jiangshi, lich, vampire, wight, banshee, and the Dullahan.

Blaze transformed into a dragon and breathed fire to see better.

Penelope whispered, "W-what's going on?" A hooded figure was sitting on a high, golden throne with emeralds.

"Your Highness, I have found some weird-looking apes," said the ghoul to the figure. "Thunder, Your Highness, we won't be unlucky! Please, Your Highness, twenty is better than thirteen."

"No, they are not living corpses!" scolded Thunder. "You could keep those silly monkeys in prison until we need them! Bloody G, you know that! Leave them there!"

At once, Clyde knew that Bloody G, who was the ghoul, was treated unfairly, but he obviously didn't care about "the weird-looking apes," so Clyde had no heart to help him. But Bloody G was obedient.

"Bloody N, Let's go!" he called in a deep voice. Bloody N, the ghost, floated to the dungeon with Bloody G. *POOF!* The Searchers of Life reappeared in prison.

"OMG!" said Penelope after the two corpses left. "First goblins, then the Oni and ogre, and now corpses! Don't be surprised if we meet Wolf-Eye... After all, it's one thing after another! Who knows how long these guys will detain us?"

Uncle Drone stood up and wiped off the dirt that got on his cloak. "Wait!" cried Blaze, realizing something. "Dad, Penelope could draw the escape!"

"Amazing idea!" whispered Uncle Drone. Penelope wrote the word "escape" on the dirt with her finger. A secret passageway showed itself.

Goldstain went down first. The passageway was crooked and old. Goldstain lowered himself to the bottom. "It's safe!" Goldstain whispered from down below. Then, Uncle Drone lowered himself down.

Clyde dropped the suitcase down, and the two men caught it then put it down. Clyde jumped into the hole, and Goldstain caught him then put Clyde down.

Penelope did the same, except Uncle Drone was the one who caught her. Kiwi jumped down and landed in Clyde's arms. Clyde let Kiwi jump again and land on his feet.

Finally, Aunt Virgo slid down the hole. When her feet landed on solid ground, the hole closed, as though it knew everyone was inside.

In the passageway, there was a hall with walls of rock. The hall was light because of the multiple candles hanging on the wall. The fire made it warm.

Because of this, Blaze felt safe enough to pull out his book. "Hmm...it says that this hall only opens to the friends of Griffin Ashford, the most powerful wizard. It is 100% safe here, and there is a bit of food.

"The meat and vegetables we brought couldn't be eaten without certain things, which we used up. Our fruit is rotten, and we only have one loaf of bread, two packs of pretzels, and a few crackers.

"There's some fresh fruit in this hall, and it's safe to stay in; I'll be cheetah form and carry Clyde, Penelope, and Kiwi for as many miles as possible. Mom, Dad, you guys fly quickly, and Goldstain can ride on one of your brooms. There is food along the way!"

Everyone agreed. But before they ran, Clyde pressed the red button on his watch, and his fainted parents appeared. "Just to make sure," muttered Clyde, getting into position.

The Searchers of Life got in position and ran. They ran for 11 hours, every now and then stopping and packing some of the magical, never-rotting fruit for later. They also stopped for a rest. Every now and then, Clyde saw chandeliers.

An hour later, the hall changed. There was a fork. "Which way should we go?" asked Clyde. Out of the two choices, one leads to the exit and the other leads to a comfortable room. There was also a riddle pinned to the wall:

Where do you people want to go?

To the exit or to a room's shadow?

To the exit, if you want, you go to "not wrong".

It might be correct, correct for long!

The other way, of course, is the opposite direction.

If you go the wrong way, think about corrections.

"So, what's the answer?" Kiwi asked Penelope. "Kiwi knows Penelope is smart!"

Penelope stared at the riddle for a long time; her friends and family were counting on her! "Left and right fork...which one to choose?" she muttered. "Synonym of 'not wrong' or 'correct' is the right direction... That's it! The exit is right! The room is left, the exit is right!"

Blaze and his parents went to the right hall. It was different. The hall was not lit by candles or chandeliers but was lit by fancy lights. The floor was paved, not rusty dirt. The walls were made of patted-in dirt, though. After an hour, they arrived at the exit. In the waves, once again.

Chapter VI
Armed with Fins

Clyde looked at the ocean before him. Where was he to sleep? Penelope drew a submarine on the wall of the exit. There was a big rocky arch.

The arch brought good luck to whoever went under it.

The Searchers of Life went under the arch and jumped into the submarine. They brought thirty pieces of fruit from the hall.

Goldstain started to drive. Although there were no windows, Clyde enjoyed watching the colorful fish swim past the submarine with his watch.

He and the rest of the Searchers of Life tried to save most of their food for later (and Kiwi ate only a small portion of a kiwi for each meal, for he had a small stomach anyway). There was plenty of water; no one knew why

Penelope drew so many water bottles at the beginning of the adventure. "Hydrated is good!" she would reply with a smile whenever Clyde bothered to ask her why.

In a submarine, there were no beds, but the Searchers of Life were flexible; they were okay with napping in their chairs.

After half an hour, Goldstain, who had never experienced being underwater, was growing seasick. "We can exchange places," suggested Uncle Drone.

Goldstain replied, "Sure, why not?"

One hour after the men had swapped spots, Clyde was in his usual spot, looking at his watch and seeing if anything harmful appeared. A purple-haired, purple-tailed mermaid showed up.

For some reason, though famous, Clyde did not know about mermaids. He thought they were harmful creatures. "It's a half-woman-half-fish monster!" screamed Clyde. "It might put us under a spell!"

"Stop it, silly goose," laughed Penelope. "It's a mermaid!"

The mermaid was swimming around the submarine, trying to tell Goldstain, the creature-understander, something.

Clyde understood the mermaid's words too, for it sounded like English. She was saying, "Want to be at the Aqua Palace?"

"What is it?" asked Clyde.

The mermaid laughed. Goldstain spoke Aqua. It was loud and raspy.

The mermaid spoke back, "Sure! We have a bunch! You guys could come now!"

Goldstain spoke Aqua again. "We have a lot!"

Goldstain spoke more Aqua, and the mermaid replied once again, "Shelves and shelves! And for food, we have fish. You guys have fruit that we don't eat. But as mermaids and mermen..."

Clyde understood. Underwater, Aqua sounds like English and without water, the voice was weird.

The mermaid blew on some powder. There was a blinding flash of light. *POOF!* The Searchers of Life were in

the water, without legs but instead with a fish tail. The
Searchers of Life liked their tails.

Clyde's shimmered with sliver and cyan. Penelope's
had pink on the top, purple on the bottom, and the two
colors blended in near the middle. Blaze's tail had black
mixed into many other rainbow colors, like a black opal.
Uncle Drone's had midnight-blue spirals, somewhat like
Vincent van Gogh's painting, The Starry Night. Aunt Virgo's
had lavender and violet stripes. Goldstain's was golden and
scarlet with a few orange sparkles. Kiwi had a tail that
looked like a kiwi. (It was hard for him to stop licking it.)

The mermaid said, "Hello, let me introduce myself.
I'm Pearl. To mermen and mermaids, I'm famous. I'm
known as daughter of Queen Coral II the Kind, the Princess
of the Sea or Pearl the Smart. I am sixteen years old. I can
understand English."

Penelope poured some Reliability Potion into Pearl's
mouth. Now, she had half as much potion she had to begin
with.

And when the mermaid announced that she was not
harmful, each of the Searchers of Life members greeted
Pearl and introduced themselves–when they were mermen

and mermaids, they could only speak Aqua and could only eat mermaid food.

"I'll lead you to the Aqua Palace," said Pearl. "Sorry for the slight delay in your Sparkle River water journey. I just want you guys to rest up."

"I guess you really are Pearl the Smart!" laughed Blaze. "How did you know where we were going?"

"I saw Wolf-Eye's ship driving past, heading towards Beijing, where his palace is. That would probably mean he was coming back from a journey. I looked at the waves behind him that the ship's engine made, and if the line keeps going backwards, it could reach Hoh campground. Wolf-Eye means no good, so he probably wanted to kill your parents, Clyde and Penelope–I saw Goldstain on Moby Dick panting and full of blood, which meant he stopped the death, but the faint is caused. Sparkle River is along the way you guys are going."

"Wow!" whispered Penelope. "Nice explanation!" Pearl led the group toward Aqua Palace. When they arrived, Kiwi gasped in excitement. The Aqua Palace was a wonderful sight!

The towers were golden and smooth. They were humongous! They were decorated with the most magnificent shells in the world.

A merman servant came and asked, "Your Majesty, who have you got with you? Prisoners? Invaders? New friends?"

"Definitely new friends, Weeder," replied Pearl, thinking Weeder was joking. "I wouldn't have opponents swimming by me uncuffed!"

Weeder, the servant, blushed. "Er, sorry, Your Majesty. Where will your new friends stay, I must ask?"

"At the East Tower. I would like it to be clean," replied Pearl. "Your prize will be a pearl."

Weeder swam into a tower with a duster.

Pearl muttered sadly, "It feels like a second ago since a poor whale was found falling from the sky."

"Moby Dick!" cried Goldstain. "Where is he? Is he okay? Is he dead?" Goldstain was not only an animal speaker but an animal lover.

"At the Hospital Dome. He should be fine, but he is badly hurt. My mom managed to somehow save him. I didn't really see how, though," Pearl replied quickly so Goldstain wouldn't be too worried.

"Phew!" said Goldstain, relieved. "He was my second friend and he carried us so far on our journey!"

"Oh, Your Majesty," said Weeder, swimming back towards Pearl, "the beds are all made, the paintings are dusted, the chairs are fixed, the stair carpet is rerolled, the railings are clean, and tables are organized neatly. And remember your promise, Your Majesty, that you'll give me one of your many pearls!"

"Make sure to bring food with Sandy and Clam," Pearl reminded Weeder. "Come," she told the Searchers of Life, swimming up towards the East Tower. The Searchers of Life followed.

Inside the tower, it was fancier than the outside.

The eight beds were very neat and matched the Searchers of Life's tails. There were beautiful paintings of sea creatures (and the portrait of a whale made Goldstain smile), the chairs were nice and sturdy (except for the rocking chairs, since they are meant to rock back and forth), and there were red carpets with no wrinkles. The railings were smooth and shiny, and the tables were exceptionally clean.

Weeder swam into the tower and asked Pearl, "Clean enough for a pearl, Your Majesty?"

"Definitely," replied Pearl kindly. She handed Weeder a big, shiny pearl the size of a mini soccer ball.

"Thanks, Your kind Majesty, but I'd better run. Queen Coral II needs me," said Weeder, swimming down the stairs. "Clam says he's preparing food–Sandy, I think, will bring it up."

"This place is quite comfortable," said Blaze, flopping down on his bed. "But tomorrow, we better keep on swimming. We can't stay here forever."

Kiwi and Clyde decided to tell mermaid jokes.

"What has beautiful hair, a pretty face, two arms, and fish's tail, looks like a mermaid, but isn't one?" asked Clyde and Kiwi replied, "A merman? No, wait. Kiwi doesn't know the answer."

"A photo of a mermaid!"

"Kiwi thinks that joke is cool! Kiwi has one too: why do mermaids know how much they weigh no matter what?"

"They weigh themselves or something?" Clyde wondered.

Kiwi asked, "With what?"

"Scales! Nice one, Kiwi! Now I get it! You're good at jokes and riddles!"

Dinner was delicious because the Searchers of Life members were mermen and mermaids. A bunch of seafood and seaweed were laid neatly on the table. The spoons were shaped like clam shells. "Yummy, yummy in Kiwi's tummy!" said Kiwi, rubbing his belly.

At 9:00 p.m., Clyde and the rest crawled into their covers. The kids yawned and closed their eyes.

Pearl looked out the window, on the lookout for sharks. She would whistle every time there was something dangerous, and mermen warriors would swim out of the W.W Dungeon until 11:30 p.m. She went to sleep with the rest of the adults.

The next day, the Searchers of Life and Pearl ate more seafood quickly and packed food to bring along. Warriors went with them, shooting harmful things, such as lionfish and cookie-cutter sharks.

Penelope would find sand to draw beds to sleep in each night. Uncle Drone and Aunt Virgo led the way, and Goldstain carried the seafood.

Blaze would turn into a dolphin every now and then and swim to the surface, looking for danger in the sky. Then, he would report his discoveries to the rest in merman mode.

Pearl would use what she knew to figure out if there were any monsters lurking in the corals. Clyde would help the warriors catch some nearby fish, if necessary.

Aunt Virgo and Uncle Drone cast safety spells on the Searchers of Life, Pearl, and the warriors if jellyfish were nearby. Whenever someone was tired, the adults would try to carry them along until they felt better.

Clyde felt armed since he could swim better than before–and the fact that there were warriors on his side.

About a day later at 11:04 a.m., the mermaids and mermen arrived at Shanghai, China. "Bye!" said Pearl sadly. "I hope I can see you soon!"

"Bye!" the others said, waving good-bye after each getting on a nearby rock at shore.

POOF!

Chapter VII
The Chest

The Searchers of Life transformed back into humans. They turned invisible so it wouldn't be suspicious to the Chinese people that there were magical beings–they might start to question them, delaying their trip. There were various buildings wherever they looked. It was crowded.

The only best way was to fly. Dragon-Blaze carried Clyde and Penelope as Aunt Virgo and Wizard-Drone flew on their brooms. Kiwi was carried by Penelope, and Goldstain sat on the back of Aunt Virgo's broom.

Whenever they got hungry, Uncle Drone would turn Goldstain (the only one out of the group who could speak Chinese) into a person who looked like a Chinese man and make Chinese money appear. Then, Goldstain would turn visible and order food at nearby Chinese restaurants. They would quickly eat and move again.

The good news was that the ride was only about six and a half hours until they reached Beijing!

"It's 5:49," groaned Blaze. His wings were sore from more than six and a half solid hours of flying. "Let's rent a hotel," suggested Goldstain, turning into a Chinese person, visible. "You guys stay invisible."

He ran off and came back. "Mutianyu Great Wall Hotel works. It's a five-star hotel!"

"Nice!" exclaimed Aunt Virgo. The Searchers of Life went into the hotel and into their room.

At dinnertime, Goldstain ordered some orange chicken and beef with broccoli. In their room, everyone turned visible again. After dinner, the kids took turns washing in the shower and changing into their pajamas. Kiwi took his bath in the sink.

Clyde, who went last out of the kids, plopped onto his bed. That day was tiring, him having to cling onto Blaze for more than six hours! Within five minutes, he fell asleep.

The grown-ups quietly washed after all three kids had gone to sleep. By 11:45 p.m., two people were on each bed, with Kiwi wrapped in a towel. Clyde had a creepy nightmare:

"I love legends!" exclaimed Dream-Clyde. He pointed to a picture of a massive monster on a poster. It was green and gruesome with razor-sharp fangs pointing up from its lower lip and long horns. "I wished they were RIGHT HERE WITH ME!" Indeed, a monster appeared. "Ah!" screamed Dream-Clyde. "What happened?" The monster grabbed Dream-Clyde and cackled, "Bwa-ha-ha-ha-ha!"

It swallowed Dream-Clyde. His lunch wailed, "No! Can this be happening?" He fell and fell and fell and fell and fell... The real Clyde woke up. That nightmare was too scary for him! He checked his watch.

It was 1:16 a.m. Everyone else was sleeping. Penelope was now the only one with her own bed—Uncle Drone and Aunt Virgo in one and Goldstain and Blaze in one. Kiwi was sleeping on the couch, the towel still engulfing his small body. Luckily, there was really no monster. Clyde tried to go back to sleep, but after one hour, he couldn't.

He decided to change and get up, not caring much that it was 2:17 a.m. He grabbed a blue long-sleeved shirt with "Clyde Suco" printed in big, white and bold letters, put it on, pulled on a pair of blue socks and dark-gray Adidas pants with black stripes, and tied his jacket around his waist. Then, he put on his sneakers. But for some reason, there was a wooden chest near the windowsill under the moonlight.

"Penelope," Clyde whispered in Penelope's ear. "Look, a chest."

It took eight minutes to wake her up. Penelope, though slept the earliest, hated sleeping the most. In a light sleep and having an excuse not to sleep, Penelope crawled out of bed to find that it was true.

"Truth or dare?" she asked Clyde, her eyes fixed on the chest. Clyde rarely chose truth.

Like usual, he said, "Dare."

"I dare you to open that chest," whispered Penelope.

Clyde slowly walked towards the chest and opened it. Penelope quietly ran to the window too. She looked at the objects inside the chest with curiosity. Clyde was mesmerized.

Inside the chest, there were two wands (one glimmering and one sparkling under the moonlight), one sword with an emerald blade that shone brightly from the stars, one shield made of diamond, arrows and a bow (the arrows with extremely sharp points), a small, sturdy helmet, and a magical blanket (no matter how cold the weather was, it would still keep you warm). There was also a silver bullet accompanied by a pistol.

Clyde grabbed the shield, and Penelope grabbed the blanket. A fire suddenly leapt up. The two kids jumped back. The fire, for some reason, did not burn anything.

The fire vanished, and a man with long, dark-brown hair appeared with a red and yellow robe on. Clyde could not believe his eyes! It was Griffin Ashford! Griffin gently whispered, "Hello, Clyde and Penelope. It is I, Griffin Ashford. This chest is for the Searchers of Life."

"But can't you help us with our fainted parents?" asked Clyde.

Griffin answered, "Stop kidding! They didn't faint! How is it possible?" And with that, he vanished.

Well, at least we know these are safe, Clyde thought. He tried to think brightly, but he still was dull about no more help. Clyde knew Griffin wasn't trying to be rude, but he was miserable that Griffin thought Clyde was lying.

Thirty-seven minutes later, Kiwi and Blaze woke up at the noise. Blaze asked, "What's that?" pointing at the chest.

Penelope replied, "Something from Griffin Ashford. The sword is for you. The helmet must be Kiwi's since it's too small for the rest of us."

Goldstain woke up too. He acted as all adults do when they are wakened, grumbling, "Keep it down!" Even friends can get grumpy. Goldstain pulled the covers over his head, revealing only a bit of his red hair.

Kiwi climbed up Clyde's back and grabbed the helmet then put it on. "Kiwi thinks this helmet is sturdy!" he exclaimed, patting it.

This time, Aunt Virgo woke up. "Keep it down!" she demanded.

She tried to go to sleep again, but when she noticed she couldn't, she decided to get up for the day. But it was 2:56 a.m.

Penelope and Blaze got dressed too, noticing most of the people were up. Aunt Virgo put on a lilac and purple robe, and black leggings, black stockings and put her folded-up cloak in her robe. Penelope put on a purple T-shirt, jeans, pink socks, and her PUMA jacket. Blaze put on a black and golden robe, gray pants, and black socks and tucked his cloak in his robe, like his mom. Then, they put their sneakers on. They kept it down, remembering Chinese people were in nearby hotel rooms.

Aunt Virgo grabbed the sparkling wand from the chest and happily muttered, "Now I have two wands!"

Clyde, Penelope, Blaze, Kiwi, and Aunt Virgo decided to plan out the rest of their journey (quietly). Twelve minutes later, they fell asleep, only their shoes off and the rest of their clothes on. After five hours, the whole Powered Group woke up.

"It's 8:08. We should eat early and set off early," suggested Clyde. Uncle Drone reached for the glimmering wand. "I have two wands now! Nice! The bow and arrow will be for Goldstain," exclaimed Uncle Drone.

He and Goldstain changed: Uncle Drone put on navy-blue robes, black pants and socks, and his cloak. Goldstain put on a red T-shirt, brown, straight pants, green socks, copper fit gloves, and a black jacket. Everyone put on their shoes.

Clyde grabbed a piece of paper and told Penelope, "Draw breakfast. It's quicker than waiting in line for food."

Penelope did as she was told and drew waffles with syrup. "We haven't eaten these since we left for our camping trip!" she muttered thoughtfully as everyone took a bite of their waffles. "It feels so good to eat these again!"

Penelope wrapped the blanket she got from Griffin around herself to see how cozy it was after she'd finished.

"YOU'RE BODYLESS, PENELOPE!" yelled Blaze.

His father hushed, "Shhh, Chinese people will get startled, okay?"

"Oh, sorry," whispered Blaze.

"Huh?" giggled Penelope. She looked at herself. She couldn't believe that her blanket turned her invisible! All three kids crawled into the blanket. That was all the blanket could hold.

Uncle Drone and Aunt Virgo turned invisible and turned Goldstain into a Chinese person to check-out. The rest followed. Clyde could hear Goldstain speaking Chinese but didn't understand. Luckily, Uncle Drone hid the gun and bullet well in his robes.

Goldstain walked towards a bathroom. "Do you need to go to the bathroom?" whispered Clyde.

Goldstain whispered back, "No, we all will turn invisible, so it would not be suspicious that I'm floating when we take flight."

In the bathroom, Uncle Drone made Goldstain back into Goldstain and made him invisible too. Out the door, Blaze turned into a dragon. The blanket slid off Dragon-Blaze's tail. Chinese people turned around, staring at the black tail, confused. Then, their expressions changed–they now seemed scared or suspicious.

Immediately, Aunt Virgo turned her son invisible. She and her husband got on their brooms. Goldstain was held by Blaze's feet. Clyde and Penelope were in the blanket on Blaze's back.

The Chinese citizens decided that the tail appeared in their vision because they were too sleepy and, only now, had they adjusted to the morning light.

Kiwi was carried by one of Penelope's hands (and Penelope's other hand gripped tightly to Blaze) while Clyde gripped both the shield and the blanket tightly, and his legs made sure he wouldn't fall.

Kiwi held the paper and pen Penelope would draw on. They flew down towards the secret door that only magical beings knew about...

Blaze gripped tighter to Goldstain, Penelope gripped tighter to Kiwi and Blaze, and Clyde gripped tighter to Blaze. Uncle Drone and Aunt Virgo gripped tighter to their brooms.

The sun shined in Clyde's eyes. The wind whistled in his ears. The crisp breeze smelled good in his nose. The chilly temperature danced outside of the blanket. It was comfortable and uncomfortable at the same time!

Penelope squinted at the distant mountains and trees. It was beautiful.

Suddenly, Aunt Virgo, Uncle Drone, and Blaze halted. They slowly flew to the ground. There were many trees and dirt. There was a very hollow Chinese fir.

"Before we continue our trip," whispered Uncle Drone, "let's stop. This is private enough to go to the bathroom if needed."

"Yes, please!" exclaimed Clyde.

Aunt Virgo waved her wands, and a stall with a toilet, trash can, sink, and toilet paper appeared in it. She, with the wand Griffin had given her, was able to make this happen. Clyde went inside and locked it.

Outside, Penelope was drawing on the dirt. She wanted to save the paper while she didn't need it. She drew a few crackers and pretzels for snacks.

Clyde finished, so he unlocked the stall and came outside. "So," explained Goldstain when he noticed, "listen carefully, kids. That rock by that hollow Chinese fir is enchanted. We must touch it together. It appeared since we felt the Dread."

Clyde understood; after all he and his friends had gone through, they were proved worthy of going to Sparkle River. That was why no one talked about taking an airplane! Clyde only didn't think of it because his family didn't buy a ticket. The Searchers of Life walked towards the rock with their hands up, ready to touch it. They touched the rock together.

They all turned visible. They were in a paved tunnel. "Before we walk any farther," Aunt Virgo warned, "get your weapons at the ready. We will be sneaking past Wolf-Eye's land. After that, we will reach Sparkle River."

Clyde held the shield up. Penelope wrapped herself in the blanket. Blaze was ready with the sword. Aunt Virgo and Wizard made sure all four wands were ready. Goldstain was ready to aim and shoot.

Together, the Searchers of Life walked to the secret door.

Chapter VIII
Werewolf Riddles

They opened it. They were able to walk half a mile until they met Wolf-Eye, cackling, armed, and with his five honest werewolf friends. The honest werewolf friends all looked the same: stringy, blond hair, small pupils in their yellow eyes, pale skin, big muscles on their arms and legs, sharp teeth and long nails, rags on their bodies and a rope tied to their waist, and a scar on the neck.

Wolf-Eye looked almost the same, except he had his blond hair combed neatly, bright-red clothes that looked cleaner than his friends' and slightly darker skin (his was like a light-peach color). He also had more muscles.

Wolf-Eye didn't trust the Searchers of Life to defeat him, so he decided to have a bit of fun by cackling, "Scraper, Rag, Furry, Moon, and Nosey. Get in your positions. Humans are foolish. Only werewolves, the true clever creatures, shall remain. Ah, food can be played with. It's fun."

The five werewolves ran far away. Wolf-Eye cackled, "The full moon is tomorrow. I can't wait!"

He vanished.

Clyde had experienced shielding since he did water balloon fights with Penelope every summer day, but he doubted that werewolves were as bad as Penelope when they would aim at him.

Blaze transformed into a cheetah. The Searchers of Life climbed on. Blaze ran at his top speed (79 mph) for thirty seconds until they came to the first werewolf, Scraper.

"My challenge," cackled Scraper, "Is to solve this nearly unsolvable riddle! If you solve it, I shall kill myself. If you do not, you die! And that means brunch." He, like Wolf-Eye, dared to risk death. It was too fake for the Searchers of Life to kill them! With Penelope on their side, the Searchers of Life realized that riddle solving was the best way to get to the river.

84

Scraper told his riddle: "Who scratches because his name means it? He has five friends! The first one starts with W and is royal! He is famous, he is. The second one has a name that sounds like the synonym of boast. The third one has a cute name, but the real him is powerful! The fourth one is the full moon, basically. The last one has a name that part of it means part of a human face that sniffs, and with it, you can smell things. Who is the person I am talking about?"

"That's easy!" exclaimed Penelope. "It's, of course, you, Scraper!"

"Grr..." growled Scraper. But he was always honest, since he and his werewolf friends had a scar. Whenever they broke a vow, the scar expanded until they died. So, the werewolf killed himself.

Blaze kept on running, but now at 64 mph. Twenty seconds later, the Searchers of Life met Rag, Furry, Moon. Furry and Moon each were standing by a door.

Rag explained, "One of my werewolves are telling the truth; one tells the lies. The scar was taken out of both werewolves for the sake of this. Tell them only one question to determine the right way. If correct, I will kill my friends and me. I still have the scar."

He did not believe that the Searchers of Life could solve this. "I've heard of this," muttered Penelope. She walked up to Furry. "If I asked Moon if the door on the left is safe for me, what would he say?"

Furry answered, "He would say, 'Yes.'"

Rag spluttered, "No! This can't be! How can they?" But of course, he still had the scar Wolf-Eye carved on his arm. He remembered that, if he broke that promise, only he would die! He didn't do anything. The scar expanded, and the werewolf died. He had sacrificed himself.

Freaking out, Blaze ran to the door on the right and ran at top speed again. Penelope was only lucky that Clyde pulled her on board before she was killed.

Forty-five minutes later, the Searchers of Life met Nosey. Nosey cackled, "My riddle you can't solve – EVER. EVER! But if you do...I shall be killed." Indeed, it was the hardest of all the riddles. Furry and Moon were far away, panting. It would take a while for them to come. Blaze needed a break too.

"Without the first two letters, I'm an intelligent mammal. Without the first three, I am a subject most schools should have. Without the first four, I am the most common English letter. What fruit am I?" asked Nosey.

He held up a bowl of fruit. "Eat the correct fruit from this bowl, and I will die. In five minutes, you guys must solve it. Or else…you guys will explode. And I would've died if I was lying."

He was almost certain that the Searchers of Life couldn't solve the riddle.

Penelope thought, "E is the most common English letter, which means five letters. Five minus three equals two. What subject has two letters and ends with E?"

Clyde warned, "Three minutes and forty-eight seconds left!" "What is it… What is it?"

"Three minutes and forty-one seconds left! But I have no idea what the answer is!"

"Oh, P.E.! Now what is an animal that's intelligent and ends with 'pe' and that's three letters long?" Goldstain thought, "Hmm…"

Clyde shouted, "Three minutes and fourteen seconds!"

"That's it, ape!" exclaimed Goldstain.

Penelope kept on thinking, "What's a fruit that ends with 'ape'? Think, Penelope, think!"

Three minutes later, Clyde screamed, "Oh no! Fourteen seconds!"

Penelope quickly got a grape in the bowl and ate it. The rest imitated Penelope and each plucked a grape from the bunch. Blaze turned into a human and then ate it.

"No!" wailed Nosey, as his head was magically chopped off.

The Searchers of Life got back on Cheetah Blaze as he started to run at 71 mph. He ran for forty-three seconds until they met up with Wolf-Eye. Furry and Moon were beside him. Wolf-Eye realized that he was wrong and had teleported his remaining friends.

The Searchers of Life got off Blaze with their weapons at the ready. Blaze transformed into a human and started to hurt Wolf-Eye with the sword. But the werewolf was tough.

Uncle Drone and Aunt Virgo shot double spells, but Wolf-Eye only had a bruise from them. Goldstain shot arrows. Wolf-Eye only had scrapes. Clyde shielded most of the kicks and punches that Wolf-Eye did. Wolf-Eye could only think of his riddle, rather than saying it.

Reading his mind, Aunt Virgo said what Wolf-Eye thought under her breath so only allies could hear: "The weakness to me, the weakness to me. Here is a hint: not related to the sea.

"Listen up, people: answer this puzzle. And the smarter you are, the better your muzzle.

"Solve this riddle, or you'll be dead in the middle: to be defeat me, find some more care, and your kicks will be stronger than a mare's.

"Make some good friends. Find kindness that never ends. Find some kisses and find some hugs, and your power will be stronger than a gazillion pugs.

"Caring for others like your father, friends, and mother will make you better than your strongest brother.

"And show the answer of this riddle. Or you'll be dead in the middle... Of your life, killed with a knife, having no wife...

"With none of the answer to this puzzle, the last thing you'll do will make you guzzle.

"The more of it the better, and none, you're a feather!"

Clyde, who was still trying to shield all the punches and kicks, asked, "Who knew such a villainous werewolf could be so...weird?" Even he already knew the answer. "Teamwork!"

Blaze had a plan. He whispered it to his friends and family, still trying to stab Wolf-Eye, "Let's do the finishing blow together." Penelope, who was now under the blanket, and Kiwi distracted Wolf-Eye.

Kiwi annoyed Wolf-Eye and ran under his legs. Penelope, invisible, poked Wolf-Eye on the back and ran when Wolf-Eye almost touched her by accident. Then, she kept on poking him.

Blaze rubbed the sword and arrows on the shield, causing friction that created sparks that eventually made the weapons catch on fire. Uncle Drone and Aunt Virgo spun all four wands around, ready to shoot a deadly spell.

Clyde signaled Penelope and Kiwi to get out of the way. Penelope and Kiwi did. Then, Penelope took off the Blanket. The whole Powered Group counted down, "THREE, TWO, ONE, SHOOT!!!"

Blaze threw the sword at Wolf-Eye's chest, Uncle Drone and Aunt Virgo shot the deadly spell, and Goldstain shot the Arrow of Fire at the same time. Right after the arrow, Goldstain grabbed the silver bullet and shot it.

BOOM! Fog prevented Clyde from seeing. It grew chilly. "Help!" cried a scratchy voice. It did not sound friendly. It sounded like Wolf-Eye. Yes, teamwork was Wolf-Eye's weakness, and especially the bullet.

"Before we get bombed ourselves, let's make a run for it! The kids need to be carried; they don't have long enough legs," ordered Aunt Virgo.

Clyde closed his eyes; even more dust was filling the air. He felt a kind arm carrying him somewhere... He couldn't make out where... He finally came back to his senses—except his eyes. They were still closed.

But Clyde could make out that he was carried by Goldstain, and Penelope was on the other arm. He could feel that there was no more dust, but he felt willow leaves brushing across his face.

As Goldstain went, it got warmer and warmer. It was cold at Wolf-Eye's, but here felt good and warm! The warmth was gradually growing, so it couldn't be the blanket since it kept a solid temperature.

He heard other people near him too. He hoped that they were friends, not Wolf-Eye following Goldstain wherever he was taking him to. Clyde thought, It feels like spring, even though I'm sure it's only summer.

Goldstain sped up. Below him, dry and dead leaves crunched and crunched and crunched.

He heard a few painted bunting birds and a bald eagle flying in the air. He felt warmth—a lot of warmth.

It was so warm; Clyde was ready to take off his jacket...but maybe he would keep it on for extra warmth while he had the chance.

He heard Penelope sighing happily because of the warmth. It was the most comfortable part of this trip.

He closed his eyes… He relaxed his arms… He allowed his head to droop… Clyde drifted off to sleep. He had a terrible dream.

"I can fly!" shouted Dream-Clyde as he soared in the air. "Who knew such a thing?"

"You're flying," muttered Dream-Penelope sadly.

Dream-Dragon-Blaze flew up but fell. This Dream-Clyde had a bad heart, so he laughed, "You can't fly! I can! You can't do anything!" He blew a raspberry at Dream-Blaze.

Dream-Penelope wanted to run and help Dream-Blaze, but she fell into a dark pit. Dream-Blaze couldn't help Dream-Penelope because something made him stick onto the ground!

Dream-Clyde continued to blow raspberries. He didn't notice Goldstain helping both injured Powered Group members. But then he could not fly either!

He was flying high at first, but he was now falling until he reached the ground…

But hard…

People were blowing raspberries at him...bruises growing on his arms...cuts expanding on his face...scratches going deeper into his legs... Punching... Kicking...

Dream-Clyde was yelling, "Save me! SAVE ME! SAVE ME!!!"

"Don't help him," said Dream-Blaze. "Why didn't he help us?"

"NO! JUST HELP ME! THAT'S SIMPLE, ISN'T IT?"

"But you didn't help us."

"BUT IT'S SIMPLE! THAT'S ALL!"

"But you're mean!"

"JUST HELP!"

"Why?"

"TO SAVE ME!"

"Why?"

"JUST DO IT!"

The evil Dream-Clyde bellowed louder, closing his eyes that were now full of blood and tears.

Something was slicing through his neck... Dream-Clyde screamed... The cut went deeper and deeper and deeper and deeper...

Chapter IX
Sparkle River

Clyde woke up. The dream was too terrible. He noticed that the heat had stopped growing. Wherever Clyde was, it was too beautiful for him.

He saw the rest of the Searchers of Life too. Blaze was carried by his dad, and so was Kiwi. And he was right: Penelope was carried by Goldstain's left arm.

There was a sparkling river with a small current. Flowers were everywhere. Bees were buzzing, and butterflies were flapping. A cardinal was chirping on a cherry blossom tree.

Goldstain put Clyde and Penelope down. Uncle Drone did the same thing but with his son and Kiwi.

Kiwi handed Penelope the paper and pen, and Penelope drew a flask. Aunt Virgo used the flask and got a bit of the water from the river, which was the River of Sparkles.

The grass was soft. Clyde decided to take a nap. He curled up in the grass and slept again. Penelope was drawing sandwiches for the Searchers of Life to eat for lunch.

The Searchers of Life (except for Clyde–he was sleeping) told Penelope their favorite types of sandwiches. "Okay," whispered Penelope. "So, it's like this. Blaze: salmon. His parents: tuna. Goldstain: tomatoes and lettuce. Kiwi wants a sandwich with kiwi, strawberries, and whipped cream, of course. I want a PB&J sandwich, and I know Clyde wants grilled cheese.

Everyone but the napping Clyde nodded. Penelope drew. Around 12:03 p.m., she finished. Clyde woke up, saw the sandwiches, and asked, "Can I please have the grilled cheese sandwich?"

"It was supposed to be for you, Clyde," replied Penelope kindly.

Kiwi exclaimed, "The fruit sandwich Kiwi has is tasty! Yummy, yummy in Kiwi's tummy!" after he took a bite of the fruity sandwich.

After everyone finished, Aunt Virgo suggested, "Let's save the flask. We go to Sparkle River and rub some of the water on us. It not only cures faints but also heals injuries."

She pointed to a nasty cut on her face that Wolf-Eye had scratched out. "This is not the most comfortable thing!"

Looking at his friends and sister, Clyde noticed that Aunt Virgo had a point.

Uncle Drone had bloody fingers, Penelope had many big bruises, Blaze had a few scrapes that were bleeding a lot, Kiwi was a bit wobbly when he stood up, and Goldstain had a black eye. The kids also had some cuts that did not heal when they tried to fight Q.C Leopardi.

Clyde didn't block a few of Wolf-Eye's attacks, so he had a deep cut on his left hand and many little cuts on his right. He followed the rest by the river and put his hands in the water.

It felt good. When he took them out, his hands were good as new! Now, Penelope had no bruise, Blaze had no scrape, Goldstain's eye looked better, Aunt Virgo had a healed face, Uncle Drone had no blood dripping out, and Kiwi could stand up very well.

98

Clyde pressed the red button on his watch. Mom and Dad appeared. Aunt Virgo poured that flask of magical water into their open mouths. Suddenly, Mom and Dad started to move again!

Clyde and Penelope hugged them tightly. Mom and Dad hugged them back. It was a sweet moment. "What happened?" asked Mom. "Where are we?"

It took a long time for the two to explain all the dangerous obstacles, how they had made their new friends, and the rest of the uncomfortable journey.

"...and so, we finally arrived here, gave you the magical water, and now you guys are back!" finished Clyde. "We even met Griffin Ashford!"

"I wished we could again," muttered Mom.

A voice said, "And so you can." Mom and Dad knew about Griffin and had been friends with him for a few years.

"GRIFFIN!!!" Mom and Dad shouted in unison, patting him on the back. "I knew you weren't killed by those goblins!" Clyde was confused. "What do you mean?"

Dad explained, "We were going on an exploration when we were young. Little did we know, goblins were there. So, we ran. But suddenly, Griffin disappeared. We thought he died—but yes, he was powerful. We hoped we could see him again. And many years later...now...we did."

"But then why didn't he help you guys, Mom and Dad?" asked Clyde.

Griffin replied sadly, "I never knew they fainted. Until now. For a decade, I was too busy to visit them. I just saw you and the Searchers of Life in China, so I thought you guys wanted to kill Wolf-Eye and claim his land as yours. That's why I gave you the weapons. I'm so sorry I didn't believe you, Clyde."

Clyde was quite forgiving. He replied, "It's okay, and we're supposed thank you."

Griffin smiled, "You're welcome."

A phoenix was flying in the air. Uncle Drone explained, "That phoenix is the Great Phoenix. He was the one who formed Sparkle River. Long ago, this place was a long hole. One day, the Great Phoenix's friends died, and he cried until the hole was full. Phoenix tears have healing powers. So that's why Sparkle River is what it is today."

Blaze smiled, "Yeah, I remember taking a history exam on that!"

Goldstain sniffed some flowers. "Wow," he grinned, "these smell like Syfacs, the flower that smells best. Beautiful too."

The Syfac was a flower with a green center and five round, sky-blue petals, and as it got closer to the center, it would get pinker.

Blaze looked at another plant and grinned. "These are definitely Barridiums. They don't smell good or bad, but they look pretty." The Barridium was a bush with flowers of countless shapes and colors. They really were pretty!

"We haven't brushed our teeth for a long time!" Clyde said, a bit worried. Griffin handed everyone a toothbrush and toothpaste.

"Thanks!" the Searchers of Life, Mom, and Dad exclaimed, grateful. They started to brush.

Two minutes later, they finished and rinsed their mouths in the river. "Sorry the weapons you gave us are lost, Griffin," apologized Aunt Virgo. It was true.

As a sympathetic person, Griffin said, "It's okay. I can recover them later, but for now, I'm taking you guys somewhere."

"Back home?" asked Clyde hopefully.

"No," replied Griffin. "It will be a surprise. Just come." Everyone did. Griffin made him, the Searchers of Life, and Clyde and Penelope's parents disappear behind touchable, seventy-degree flames.

They reappeared in a mansion. Griffin pointed to a button. "This," he explained, "is a button that will teleport you guys to wherever you want if you press it! This place is your new home. I moved all your belongings here. This is the money from selling your homes."

He handed Mom and Uncle Drone some money each; Uncle Drone's money looked different than his sister-in-law's: he had two golden cubes with the name Voltix Ashford, a silver ball with the name Crash Starcue, five bronze ingots with the name Mist Ko, and a few blue coins with runes showing. "Everything has something good."

The first few days, Clyde spent his time exploring. He discovered that there was a Healthy Tiramisu Cheesecake Room! He loved it here.

102

During the night of the sixth of August, Clyde finished the fancy food he got and went into the elevator. He pressed the "up" button. He went up...up...up... *BEEP!*

The elevator stopped. The doors opened, and Clyde walked out. He walked down the hall and saw three doors. He opened the door in the middle and walked into his room. He pulled open another door that led to the Kids' Bathroom (aka the KB). Like everywhere else in the mansion, the KB was fancy.

Blaze and Penelope were already brushing their teeth. Out of the nine toothpaste flavors, Clyde decided to use strawberry-flavored toothpaste. Blaze used peppermint, and Penelope used bubble gum. The other flavors were cotton candy, chocolate, watermelon, honey, lemon, and blueberry.

After they finished brushing their teeth, Blaze and Penelope got out of the KB to their own rooms so Clyde could shower. Clyde took off his clothes and turned on the shower. Then, he stepped in.

Blaze and Penelope met up in Blaze's room. The head of his bed was like a dragon's head, and the foot was like a dragon's tail. His walls were painted black, and the windows had a beautiful view of Goldstain's new garden!

The two sat at the fancy desk, talking about who should go next. "Maybe you," replied Blaze. "I'm born on December 14th, 2008, but you were born on April 11th, 2009. I'm a little older, so I can sleep a little later."

They agreed to Blaze's plan. Just at that moment, a clean Clyde with a fancy, green towel wrapped around him opened the door and told his sister and cousin, "I finished." Then, he scurried off to his own room. Penelope went into the KB and took her shower.

When Clyde was finished changing into his pajamas, he walked into Blaze's room and exclaimed, "You can come to my room!"

Blaze replied, "Wait a sec." He grabbed a book from a shelf that was carved with dragons on them and followed Clyde.

Clyde opened the door to his room. He and Blaze each sat on a beanbag chair. "I just thought we could talk a bit," Clyde explained. Blaze handed the book to Clyde: Magical Creature Explore's Guide.

"For me?" asked Clyde hopefully.

"Yes, it's for you," replied Blaze. "You were the one who found the chest. You are the son of the best friends of Griffin Ashford. That's why we're at this beautiful home."

"Thanks!" Clyde shouted repeatedly. He looked at the book's mysterious signature. "But who wrote this?"

He stared at the "X22-6•D1-7" for a long time.

Penelope came in, already changed. Blaze ran into the KB and took his shower. Mom and Dad came in. "Goodnight, kids," they whispered.

Penelope ran back into her own room with Mom as Dad tucked Clyde in. Clyde was extremely excited about his birthday–it was tomorrow! Blaze finished washing and went into his own room. He, too, was tucked in.

Clyde listened and watched the big, fat raindrops gently fall onto the ground meters below. The leaves rustled in the wind outside. He watched the sun slowly set behind Goldstain's new apple orchard.

This beauty caused his head to droop and his eyes to relax... They closed in only a few seconds.

Chapter X
Happy Birthday!

The next morning, Clyde woke up, expecting someone to shout, "Happy 9th birthday, Clyde!" but no one did. He pulled on his favorite outfit: a green T-shirt and gray sweatpants.

He walked into Penelope's room, but she was not there. He walked into Blaze's room, but he was not there. He walked into the KB, but no one was there.

Clyde decided to go into the elevator, and he pressed the "down" button. A few minutes later, the doors slid open, and there was a fork. He took the left fork. Then, there were two doors.

Clyde peeked at both. His parents were not in any.

He walked back then took the right fork. There were three doors. He first looked in Goldstain's room. His walls were red and golden. But his bed had no Goldstain.

Clyde peeked at Aunt Virgo's then Uncle Drone's. But no one was in any. He went to the elevator, pressed the "down" button, and arrived at the next floor. He walked to a green door, opened it, and looked around for Kiwi, who was not there.

He went to the elevator again, pressed the "down" button, and arrived at the breakfast table within a minute. The doors slid open, and Clyde stepped out.

At his seat, there was his breakfast: eggs, broccoli, and bacon. But other than that, he saw only Penelope, who shouted, "Happy Birthday, Clyde! I also know who wrote the Magical Creature Explorer's Guide!"

"Who is it?"

"The author is Voltix Ashford, Griffin's great-great-great-great grandfather! X is the end of Voltix; D is the end of Ashford! V is the start of Voltix, and the twenty-second letter of the alphabet. Pretty much the same, but with A. There are six letters in Voltix, yet seven in Ashford.

"Yay," muttered Clyde unhappily. He still wanted cake. He nibbled his breakfast and walked into the elevator.

As the doors slid open, Clyde walked in and pressed the "up" button. He went up and up and up...

DING!

Clyde arrived on the fifth floor. He walked out and ran into the hallway. He heard another elevator ding, but he did not care who it was. He stopped walking. It's just going to be a terrible birthday, that's all, he thought.

He heard footsteps near him, but he didn't want to see who was there. When there were no more footsteps, Clyde continued walking down the hallway.

He opened the door to the right of him and sadly walked inside. It was the Healthy Tiramisu Cheesecake room. At least he could eat as much cheesecake as he wanted!

But he noticed that the great chandelier was not on like it used to be. Suddenly, the lights turned on and the Searchers of Life, Mom, and Dad shouted, "Happy 9th birthday, Clyde!" Clyde jumped. He'd never had a surprise party before!

Dad held up a cake and explained, "Ice cream cake plus tiramisu cheesecake equals a great birthday!"

Goldstain put the candles on the cake and turned off the lights again. Everyone sang, "Happy birthday to you! Happy birthday to you! Happy birthday to Cly-yde, happy birthday to you!" Then, they cheered as Clyde made a wish and blew out his candles. His wish was that he could have all his birthdays like this.

Mom cut the cake and gave everyone a slice–Clyde with the biggest. Everyone also "dove" into the tiramisu cheesecake. It was the best birthday of Clyde's entire life.

Aunt Virgo and Uncle Drone let the balloons they blew up earlier rise to the ceiling. Confetti fell from the ceiling. There was also a piñata. Clyde was the only one who managed to break it blindfolded.

Candy sprinkled all over the kids. There were also fortune cookies in the piñata. Clyde read his fortune. "This fortune says that my old friends will meet me again."

His BFF, Avery, wasn't in the same class as him for two solid years! Did this mean Avery will finally be in the same class as Clyde? Clyde sure hoped so. He decided to play his other birthday games. He played Pin the Tail on the Donkey, which he was good at.

Clyde managed to pin the tail on the donkey's hind legs.

It was too fun for Clyde. Then, after everyone got a turn, the Searchers of Life, Mom, and Dad decided to see who could eat their doughnut the fastest with no hands.

Clyde was 3rd to finish (Blaze was 1st, mainly because he transformed into a dragon, so he had a bigger mouth).

Kiwi was last since he had the smallest mouth, but he was completely okay with it since he was the one who managed to pin the tail on the donkey.

Then, Clyde unwrapped his presents: Penelope gave him a sticky hand, Blaze gave him a Lego dragon, Aunt Virgo and Wizard gave him glow-in-the-dark pencils, Goldstain gave him a pair of binoculars, Kiwi gave him a yoyo, and Mom and Dad gave him a card and a box of toys that had Clyde always wanted.

Clyde loved all these presents. It was so fun!

Three weeks later, Clyde was with Mom. She pressed the teleporting button, and she and Clyde were teleported to Staples, in the bathroom (so it wouldn't look weird of they suddenly appeared out of nowhere).

Together, the two found pencils, erasers, pens, paper, a notebook, scissors, glue sticks, and markers for Green River Elementary, a private school run by Dad.

A few meters away, Penelope and Dad were finding Penelope's supplies. A few shelves back, Blaze was with his parents, finding materials for Magician Hills Academy, which was located by a secret river.

Together, they walked to the parking lot. Goldstain's golden car was waiting for them. It was large so everyone could fit. They sat down, and Goldstain pushed a button. ZAP! They teleported back with their supplies.

Clyde suddenly started to worry. Would he be in the same class as Penelope as usual? Would his enemy, Zilla, see him often? These terrible thoughts overwhelmed Clyde. Did the first day of school have to be so challenging? Why did Zilla have to attend Green River Elementary?

He didn't feel better after he noticed Penelope thinking about the same things. She was circling around with a worried look on her face. Every time she thought of worse possibilities, she would pace around quicker and have a more worried look on her face.

Goldstain noticed and firmly whispered, "Everything will be okay." Clyde hoped Goldstain was correct, but he didn't feel any better.

That night, he looked at his dinner: milk and pepperoni pizza. Although pizza was his third favorite food, he didn't eat it. When he noticed that it the date was August 31st, his stomach made a lurch.

Penelope tried to comfort Clyde, but since she was worried about the same thing, Clyde didn't feel better.

"Uh, tomorrow is Saturday, which means the next day is Sunday, and after that it's Labor Day. Three more days to wait!" explained Penelope. She didn't make herself comfortable with her words.

It was Blaze that made the Suco kids feel better. "Think about it," he exclaimed, "you haven't seen your best friends for two months! Don't bother looking at the cons of school. Think on the bright side!"

Clyde knew Blaze had a point.

What if he was in the same class as Penelope? What if Avery (like in the fortune) was in the same class as him?

Clyde was quite lucky that his BFF attended the school he did.

These thoughts made Clyde excited for school. He finished dinner quickly and didn't even go for seconds. He rushed into the elevator and went up. Then, he did his nightly routine.

He got into his pajamas quickly and went to bed early. Sadly, Penelope reminded him that the first day of school was on September 4th, so Clyde stayed up until 1:42 a.m.

On September 4th, Clyde woke up. He rushed to the elevator, pressed the "down" button, and ran to his seat as soon as the doors slid open.

He gobbled his French toast quickly; he didn't even bother to add syrup. He packed so quickly that his arms were a blur.

Clyde quickly got ready to leave. Mom held Clyde and Penelope's hands. Clyde pressed the Teleporting Button. ZAP!

They teleported to the back of a trce in Green River Elementary.

"Good luck!" whispered Mom. Zilla walked by and saw Clyde. Clyde hoped Mom was behind him, but she wasn't. Zilla was in fifth grade already.

Clyde gulped. Zilla laughed, "Your backpack is terrible! It looks like a worm with big ears–" Zilla ran off as soon as she saw a few parents of fifth graders. She could not let anyone see that she didn't like Clyde. Clyde scowled, "Zilla, it's obviously a king cobra!"

A few minutes later, Clyde found himself in a classroom. He sat down on a seat in the front row and saw Avery settling down on a chair to the right of him. Penelope was ready to start class at the seat left of Clyde.

Clyde couldn't believe that he was so lucky!

Across the hall, Zilla found herself in her new classroom. She scowled when she saw that she hadn't brought her backpack.

Mr. Karm, her teacher, told her that for forgetting her backpack would result in getting detention for a week, even if she remembered tomorrow.

Penelope was wondering what jokes she should share with the class at recess. Avery told Penelope quietly, "Pay attention."

Penelope quickly looked up.

Ms. Reat, a kind teacher whom Dad had hired, greeted everyone. "Good morning class," she exclaimed sweetly. "Let's take attendance! Let's start with Philip!"

"I'M HERE!!!"

"Ricardo!"

"Here!"

"Lucy!"

"Here!"

"Ken!"

"Here!"

"Helen!"

"Here!"

"Matthew!"

"Here!"

"Dorothy! Hmm...doesn't look like she's here yet..."

She continued to take attendance. Clyde heard Avery's name called: "Avery!"

"Here!" replied Avery. Then, he heard, "Clyde!"

Quickly, Clyde said, "Here!"

Avery's last name was Smith, and since Clyde's was Suco, they were next to each other on the alphabet.

"Penelope!"

"HEAR!" shouted Penelope, pointing at her ear.

"And Leo?"

"I'm here, and I'm always on time as you know, and I'm never tardy, not even in your d–"

"–That's enough, Leo. Thank you for sharing, but it's best if you share at Show and Tell. Okay, finally, Maya! Oh, she and Dorothy aren't here yet."

Just at that moment, Dorothy and Maya opened the door to the classroom with Mr. and Mrs. Valdez. "Dang, we're late," panted Maya.

"I wished we were as punctual as Leo," said Dorothy.

Maya muttered under her breath so Leo wouldn't hear, "He has a big mouth."

"Here are your seats, girls," Ms. Reat pointed to a seat behind Ken and a seat to the right of Ricardo.

But both Dorothy and Maya wanted the seat to the right of Ricardo (the front row).

The girls did "Rock Paper Scissors," and since Maya won, she could sit in the front row. Dorothy wasn't too happy with the results.

After that, Ms. Reat happily sang, "It's Show and Tell! Who wants to go first?"

Ken and Clyde's hands were first, but Ken wavered while he raised it. Ken was in the same class as Clyde since Kindergarten.

"Ken, you may go first. You can be next, Clyde." Ken walked up to the front of the class.

"This is my new watch," he explained. "I got it last month! It's special to me because...well...it was expensive. Um, I got it on August 2nd this year for, like, a present."

He walked back to his seat. "Uh, Clyde, I think it's your turn."

Clyde grinned. He knew exactly what he should share: his amazing vacation of survival.

- The End -

About the Author

Karina W. Zhang is a fourth grader and an author of kids' fantasy books. She is also a rhythmic gymnast, a ballerina, and a music composer. She loves any school subject that sparkles creativity, such as Writing. She authored this book during the Coronavirus pandemic in 2021. Since she was isolated from her friends, she decided it would be a good idea to take an imaginary journey with them. Each member of the *Searchers of Life* matches the personality of someone Karina knows.

You can visit her online at www.karinazhang.me